T0306499

WHAT THINGS ARE

AGNIESZKA STUDZINSKA

WHAT
THINGS
ARE

 **EYEWEAR** PUBLISHING

First published in 2014
by Eyewear Publishing Ltd
74 Leith Mansions, Grantully Road
London w9 1lj
United Kingdom

Typeset with graphic design by Edwin Smet
Author photograph Andy Bullock
Printed in England by TJ International Ltd, Padstow, Cornwall

WWW.EYEWEARPUBLISHING.COM

For
Maja, Jozef and Richard

Agnieszka Studzinska
was born in Poland in 1975.
She has an MA in Creative Writing from UEA.
She has worked as a freelance researcher in
broadcasting, an English teacher and is now
an editor of a community magazine in West
London. Her work has been previously
published in *Agenda*, *Wolf* and by Eyewear.
Her debut collection *Snow Calling*
(Salt) was shortlisted for the London
New Poetry Award 2010. She lives in
London with her husband
and two children.

Table of Contents

I

II

III

I

All human actions have one or more of these seven causes: chance, nature, compulsion, habit, reason, passion, and desire.

Aristotle

Bird Confidence

I can almost touch your beak as it opens,
leaves wrestling with our shadows.
You skit from one branch to another
unafraid of the garden's obscurities.
Between the limbs of the tree
you find what you want –
from where I am, you darn the air
mending the gap we shape as you fly,
I stand still –

Lake

To the far left, a group of teenagers holler.
It's summer and their skin is inside the lake's

cool luring body as they play in its grey-green
dusk – limbs – like reeds entwined in the lake bed.

I touch my husband's shoulders, edges
of land from which I dive – swim through

the reef and burrows of what we had made,
listening to young distant cries breaking.

Grass

With our children behind us playing,
              we sit next to each other, heads touching.

The grass is callow, summer soft & somewhere
              in the distance we can smell where it's been cut.

Shavings of green blades stick to our clothes
              the sky to our flesh, goosebump blue.

When the children return, we open our arms to theirs
              but I can still feel you, faintly pressing for more.

Cicadas

They swerve to get to the grass, a heavy fall on a drained road,
keeling across the weight of each shell, desperate.

It's mating season and their urgency is muscled in my head
as I think of my teenage years, that boy in the park, grey eyes,

our tongues like leaves, everything burying itself in my skin,
digging for more, blue air by the sycamore tree.

The clicks of the cicadas in the lemon groves strum
close to this baked ground on which I sit in a lemon light

and think of what might have been, if anything at all,
how different each shade of lemon hangs on relenting branches –

Praying Mantis

The origami of this flesh
twisted sheaths of green,

our bodies on the stairs
luminescent in sweat

as I grasp my forelegs
like a praying mantis

unable to let go, imagine
through the avenues of an afternoon

in a neon of rain, two creatures –
one biting off the head of another

and us in this primal flourish,
being eaten of meaning.

Stinging Nettles

The burning –
the slow tide of yellow,
a prickle expanding
to a thousand needles
gracefully entering
the surface of us,
then deeper
layering the bone
with feathered spines
that spread their softness
to a spur of deception,
the burning –
the surprise of it,
how easily it stings
our flesh.

Daffodils

It has taken an afternoon for them to open,
        all but one, at the centre of the bunch

yellow with disquiet, unpronounced,
        unwilling to emerge for this world,

it's waiting patiently, the way you did
        to get me back – reclaim what *was*.

I turn off the light, open the curtains,
        watch dusk, translucence, bring you home.

Scar

A hairline crack seams your left wrist
as you move your arm above your head,

a broken wing suspended – light swoops
this room like swallows darkening the sky.

I think of things I haven't told you
& things you might have withheld.

Is knowing each other knowing all of each other?
Is that knowing? Is that called love, or *in* love?

Or something else entirely?

In bed that night, your arm went through
my arched legs & pulled me closer.

Interior

I watch him from the bed
                    sitting in the armchair
his thumb playing the pages of a book.

The night city is musk
                    pivots on darkness
broken by street traffic.

I lose myself in the ribcage of his body
                    as he coils in the fabric
of what matters and finally writes –

          a present from the city split in half
sometimes when things fall, they fall into place.

Through an open window
                    the city is swaying in conversations
but all we can really hear is the car alarm,

the shrill of its pitch, continuous
                    until something's dislodged.

Ocean Sleepers

On that holiday, we were too drunk to ride the motorbike
back to our apartment as darkness removed itself from dawn

and forced us to sleep on the beach that night, on deckchairs,
muscles of water around us – tightening – the smell of salt

on our jackets. It was not freedom, as I had thought back then,
the chilled breath of the sea, the indifferent expanse of the sky

we had stared at, consciously, wilful of its endless mark.
In the morning, the deckchair man shooed us off as we walked

on dappled sand back to the knowledge of being in love
with someone *wrong* or the word itself *wrong*,

its edges of shell against my ear, listening – washing out to sea.

Storm

The morning lake was a broken vertebra,
            fish razored the blue bones of water,

a sky chalked –
          the olive groves we visited yesterday
             uneasy.

That evening at the restaurant,
          we ate our food observing the moonlight
             swing
from behind the mountains,
              imagined village life –

in the distance – we could hear the storm
                as it turned over the earth,
receding from where we were.

Rain

for Richard

Like a scuttle of bird beaks then a full pelt
against the window, as I lie there thinking
of the dead fledgling my cat brought in –
veined & transparent like a single droplet of rain
& I picked it up with a shovel, put the dead bird
in the dustbin & the rain erasing the streets &
somewhere someone caught under – I can almost
hear the wet voices – on the outskirts, on the peak
of where they stood, half laughing like that time
in Greece, at the top of a hill, both of us drenched.
Sometimes, I look at that photograph we asked
a stranger to take & think how happy we looked,
how knowing of love we were, even at the very end
of it – luminous –

Ladder to the Moon

after Georgia O'Keeffe's painting 'Ladder to the Moon'

I could drown in this twilight, if it wasn't for your hand
or the ladder to the moon. In my mind, I climb the ladder

and from this angle stare at us below. Up here, the moon
is callous, stars barbed as if to protect them from anything

coming too close. The night sky is a raven, we are lost
in its wing as we stare upwards, eavesdrop on its silence

as it culls the gasp of the sea, the fragile fish bones of thought.
We are scalloped like a shell in a bed as we listen to innocence

in the gully of the night, the sea now speechless and wild.

Horses

Necks like mountain slopes dipping into a valley.
They look lost in the silent light of sleep,

horse skin smooth against horse skin.
Suddenly they buckle and we are left watching

a field of winter. Sometimes in bed, I can feel
your arm reaching towards me, snow galloping

outside and this time the horses remain still,
their breath in my mouth, their power overwhelming.

Saturday

It's late winter and the weather is not as it should be,
the day disguised in so many ways –

I am walking on the edge of the pavement as if
it was a frozen stream, careful of my balance –

the shopping bags heavy – suddenly a man I had known
fifteen years ago stands before me, our sudden exchange –

how are you? I can't believe it's…?
the flashback of our laced bodies on that one night,

coiled and uncoiling spreads in the middle of the High Street
and the snow sheds its white fall, my lungs working harder,

the whirl of the air like a bridge we pass over or under,
or never at all –

At the end we kiss so easily, the way friends do,
as if we were going to see each other again, as if nothing happened.

Anniversary

The sun files through the shutters, spring –
I move through our bedroom semi-naked

like a stream of shadow flitting across the furniture
as I touch all our things – this stuff we've collected –

You stand behind me, by the chest of drawers,
tracing the map of my back to the top of my neck,

as if connecting each bone in my spine back to my body –
I want to turn around, tell you what I'd like you to do,

lose myself in the brilliance of the morning, but you are going
to work, so I say *have a good day, call me later* –

the blossom stuck to your shoes, the blossom in my lap like a head.

The Stag in the Snow

For all that we can't say,
the need to be close
to the very thing we can't touch.

II

Silently the birds fly through us. O, I who long to grow,
I look outside myself, and the tree inside me grows

Rainer Maria Rilke

Childless

Along the fence between its boards,
the Campanula swims into the wood.

The rain sheds its thick tragic pour,
loosens the bloom free.

All that divides must join again,
so you watch the blushing and tightening

of foliage in seasons, how it retracts
to a knuckle of hardness in your throat.

Scan

If I look closely, I see a mouth like a whisper,
hollow eyes, the suggestion of a body.
Week by week, I engulf two geographies
as you move inside me when I least expect it,
remind me how fragile this could be –

                    water, blood, bone.

I am silted by this river you've made
copper-red, sable and ready to flood.

Contraction

I find the scrap of paper in a gardening book,
my husband's penciled writing of the timings

between each stretch of sunken waves:
16.09 – strong, 16.14 – mild, 16.24 – mild,

16.31 – mild, 16.43 – strong – until at 19.51
the swell inside my stomach moved quickly.

I read the language of these numbers,
like a lost letter, the subtle pattern and accuracy

of this *maths* defining those grey hours before
the world dilated and we entered together –

wet and adrift, our footing jolted, the air in our lungs
different, eyes unadjusted to saline light –

and the paper-note as a reference tucked away
like a pocket watch stopped in its precision and making.

Emergency

I hold her between hip & breastbone,
watch the tidy outpouring of water from a running tap
as I slit its current with a glass & then she stiffens,
flops to one side & shakes, eyes rolling back
as if all the sunlight she has known has entered her body
& won't let go. I clutch her with all the water left in mine
& run down the hallway, opening the door, calling
her name as if she was running too fast in front of me,
ignoring the things I had not yet managed to tell her
& the neighbour's gate is too stiff & I push & push,
yelling so hard that the veins on my face break like a web
tearing the threads between us –
I heard someone say,
get her to theatre, keep pushing. How I pushed for you then
in your resistance to enter – wild kicking
like that of my foot on the gate, the word *ambulance*
stitching the air & my neighbour in the background
& you somewhere watching us all, crouching on the floor
as if we were looking for something that we couldn't
recover or claim as our own, not ever – not truly –
I thought how fragile an afternoon always is,
your body slowing as the sun clipped us all
& the paramedics saying *she's OK*
as the hurtle of crying brought you back
unlike the first time, when you entered silently,
an odour of snow on skin.

Dog Woman

after Paula Rego

The leaded greys of pencil and charcoal
are cross-hatched waters rupturing,
her mouth opens to the beast in us.
She howls at first gently like a wolf
as the moon opens wider over
all the animals in the depths of night.
I open every pore in my voice,
every sound in my hunched body,
sweat turns into clouds carrying
the weight under my hips into morning air.
And the night fox crosses the road,
a vole in his mouth, snapping flowers
underfoot, the urgency of his hunger
is the dog woman, my own catch
as he swims, all pewter to my chest
whimpering for food.

Snowfall

Your voice, a dart, strikes each corner of the room,
demanding in your rawness, like the snow that fell

this morning. Everything is safe for a few hours as I hold you,
snow-sifted, velvet, and look at the tracked bird prints

in the neighbour's garden, the wheelbarrow turned upside down,
the snow-filled shoes, frosted sweepings, a ball under a shrub,

the snow-lined branches of a fig tree stretching to the tips
of the white, tongue-tied air, the shovel leaning on the fence ready.

What Things Are

Fingers in every direction, soft tongue: *dat-dat*
you say, to what is familiar & new.
You don't have the words to classify or judge,
free of language, everything is interchangeable
even love of which you only know one kind,
unaware of failure or how one kiss can mean
so many things. Slowly, you will learn to confine
this world & what you'll see, you will interpret
what you believe it to be, like the rest of us
in this fallible space & the world will be yours
to work out, willing you to learn.

Pear

Today, you have learnt to say *pear*
pear, pursing your lips & like a pip
spitting the word onto a blank floor.
There, it's out now –
& tomorrow? What will you discard?
What sequence of matter? Which gift?
What figment of our rationale –
pear, it rolls like –
unlatches, falls from your mouth
& I look at what you've dropped,
pick it up.

Orchard

The orchards are not in blossom, a boulevard
of hunched figures their branches knuckled,

the bark buried – pathways of graceless shapes,
though they burgeon year after year in this field,

like a village mother with her children,
unshakable beauty – apple after apple

falling from the tree – I watch you
trying to catch them in my mother's garden,

play with three of them, letting one by one
roll away and you watch me hide them from you.

We play like this all morning, mother & daughter,
until the warmth sends us for shade

as we lie on grass below the apple branches,
below their gloaming –

Rage

It comes as fast & sudden as a hailstorm
a small trigger from her non-compliant tone,
earthy & turfed as she answers *No* or from her stare
as biting & steady as our love & I have no control
then, over her or anything – how utterly lost we are –
in so many ways no longer mine but always mine &
when she says, *mummy you put the words in my body when
you made me*, I think of those long nights of crafting –
words we'd used, language shedding its bark,
the violet black of the mind,
the powdered grey of her speech –

Milk Tooth

In the bathroom mirror our reflections collide,
you brush your teeth & I the air that makes us.

As if a sea storm had washed up the one tiny
bone in the wave of your hand as it shows

me a small tooth covered in blood & toothpaste,
a token of the distance you have travelled so far

& so quickly. We put the tooth under a pillow
in the calm sea full of shadows & more bones.

Dandelions

Once in a field of dandelions
you called the seed heads *bubbles*
as you blew each one naked
chasing them as they streamed upwards
escaping your grasp & in your delight
you were oblivious to everyone.

I like your game of hide-and-seek,
its intangible logic – all eyes on you
& your hands covering your face
so that you are invisible & all
that you want to erase is possible.

If I shut my eyes, really tight,
just like you, could I be where you are?
Join your dandelion-bubble world
wherever that is & the scattering
of those seeds from the floret
triumphantly falling, embedding earth.

Owlet

I sway to the heartbeat of an owlet
that flies around me, tapping
at the window with its beak,
how different we are – how the same –
under cracked pores little owl faces
blemish my skin, owl feathers line the floor
like reels of thread unfastening
ready to stitch my own pair of wings
as yours widen in the attempt to leave.

III

Now is never then. Now is always now. Even then is now.

Ann Ambrecht

Nesting

I

As the magpie picks the veins of the earth,
we salvage what is left from your parents' house.

That summer we watch our daughter run across
this garden marking her shadow in ours –

in the shimmering pivots of light rain
in the sun's bones, she runs on every synonym

for memory, treading it down as she moves
                              in and out
from the garden and into the house
                              back out again
a wire of birds across the pit of sky
a silhouette of dust trailing around her

dust in our throats – spaces of dust to be cleaned.

II

Our new family house whispered us in – a March arrival.
I remember the kitchen, sun immersing the floors,
those slackening sounds of footsteps and opened windows
letting the light pave the contours of light. Someone else's
daffodils flowering in the garden, someone else's presence rippling,
the newsprint from the fish & chips of that night's dinner
around us like tumbleweed. We scrubbed, painted, our smell
soon became the new smell – our own dust settling.

III

The air tasted black, it was the only air.
The black of concrete embossed on your flesh
and held you upright for a little while and the breath
of the walls blew you away to a corner and the walls
at the end could no longer take what they contained.
A black house made of bones.
A sister and a brother somewhere inside camouflaged –

IV

When our daughter had finished the last purl of her running
housed your memories in the cornflour blue of *that* garden –

we sat there looking at rows of lavender, the yew tree, hydrangeas,
the agapanthus we uprooted to take with us and replant

in our own new garden – all of your mother's diligent work –
listened to the changed silence of stripped bloom.

V

In this village a swallow of men circle outside a house –
a taupe morning and there is drink in their hands.

Constancy of village life like a moonbeam holds them in place –
What might have been and what has been, point to one end.

They are not in a hurry. The day has no expectations. Some lean
unadorned on a wall – they are the wall – the mortar –

they are here whistling like the heat in the summer months
at the stray dogs that slumber – unpredictable, beside them,

like the mind – how quickly it turns, like the dogs
never too far away from danger – homeless.

VI
Two women lean out from the windows of the fourth floor,
their poultry-white arms pressed on the sills, faces strayed

in the air of yet another late-afternoon conversation.
Somewhere the clatter of plates like clocks striking

reminds everyone that it's supper and the village gets ready.
The balconies overlook the playground and on them duvets

hang full of winter dust and buried sleep. A mother
repeatedly shouts down to her children – her tongue

weary, blown in the flurry of effort and task
her children's voices marbled, their echoing feet in flight

and the day slipping away like shade against the sun-blanched wall,
separating
                    one block of flats
with another –

VII

The house is already half dead like a wounded bird –
my grandmother between its bricks flickering,

somehow – everything inside the house becomes less *hers*
as time moves forward, though it is *hers, it is hers*, we say.

For the winter they move her elsewhere, too cold to stay
here, though she wants to stay – collect, make it more *hers*

as she disappears slowly – make it *ours* again.

VIII

The strength of the wind has rounded,
spring is here again –
sensing the new space we inhabit.
I think of the architecture of family,
how our children play 'house' in this home now,
how a house stands over centuries in tawn-lights of seasons,
watching like an old oak in a field.

Boat

Our son climbs into our bed like an oar that has slipped
from its boat, sometimes, I come to bed & find him
already there – a throwback of his father, asleep
& handsome. On some nights our daughter comes in –
bodies like briar, a river below & I know that this midnight
rowing won't last – the overture of this love shifted,
like a surge of stars in the river itself, our boat mooring.

Drawing

My daughter's art is on the kitchen walls, hieroglyphs –
this morning she surrounds herself yet again with crayons,

has strayed into her drawing – almost irrevocable
as she casts away the delicate existence of one place,

nets the likeness of how she sees the world and shows me
a house with a yellow roof, flowers, almost as big as the house,

rain falling neatly out of the sky in two lines, grass so perfect
that it's impossible to imagine any house standing

on such tranquillity –

February

We garden under the early rise of the moon, its scythe-like shape
a gentle reminder of how long we have. You cut the branches

of a tree and we all help to move them, working like a colony,
even the little one drags a branch like a dead body across the grass.

You keep cutting until we see a concrete flow of path, the garden's
galaxy gathering us in channels of quiet until it breaks with the flock

of geese like ellipses across the sky. The noise of their migration
distracts us as we follow their flight –

October

after 'October' 1961 by Roger Hilton

Something has slipped
        the lines subside
blindly locking each other
        distorting our way of seeing,
they founder like my daughter's
        drawings of things coming
together   awkward
brown-black of blood that joins us
the two red lines
       never quite
          linking
the white stamp of an autumn sky.

It's surprisingly hot for October
   the days, almost transparent
like the moon or a scan
        of a smaller moon,
disappearing in the background
       as the body keeps turning
moving away like my father who dissolves
       in the very grain of the paper
he is at the core of the painting
        on the edge,
you can see him   just there,
his foot stepping away.

Sand in November

Is somehow lighter on this winter beach,
foot-beaten. Cloud light. It's softer –

more impressionable and forgiving
as we move through it like sapped

wind, our children moaning
and the day like a tide, curling

further away. We are all inside out
like the oddities the sea offers,

abandons – a caged light lengthening
across the sand as I walk faster,

air slowing us down,
I am trying, really trying –

Rooftops

It has not stopped raining since our arrival
at this family cottage near the sea. Before
the moon appears, it's still light enough to see
the rooftops from our windows, the slate, silvered
with the sheen of dusted rain, barely visible –
constant. The children sleep upstairs and you
with them, tired and far away. I sit downstairs
between these rooftops, watching their slant –
I think I can hear the splinter of firewood,
the rasp of the moonlight, shimmers of a town
dreaming, the bats hanging on their threshold.

By the River

I sit in a car reading,
the river's brown belly before me
under the equally dull sky flowing slowly,
or so it seems at first and I am caught
between the book, a view and the knowledge
of how things change –

In a minute, I will turn this scene,
pick you up from playschool
take us home, where you will point
to my wedding photograph in the hallway,
say *I wasn't in this world then mummy*.

I think of the river then,
rising, flooding, tunnelling towards
the sea, its mountainous waves
billowing, becoming –

Visiting

The winter moon shone in the smoke of nightfall
and the snow took all our words as we stood there,

daughter and father or what we remembered
of ourselves as daughter and father, something

else now. I tightened my coat, the one my mother
wore at her wedding, folded myself in her body,

out again in my own as you took my arm and I
followed your footsteps to the blocks of flats,

up an elevator, the metal pull shuddering as it took
us higher – closer than we had ever been –

when you opened the door, supper waited,
all the years of not eating together on a plate,

as if to say, tell me –
what can you possibly tell me, where do we start?

Father

The table by the window overlooks the courtyard with the empty swings and the dog that runs around the bench as if he was chasing a ghost bird; I glide my hand across the oilcloth with overlapping marks of lemon tea as you sit cross-legged with a cigarette ignoring the smoke like a summer fly while the sun drenches the kitchen and the flower you placed on the table treads water, bends a little, wallpaper behind me, sheer, where light has beaten against it like a heart, day in day out, my head leaning against the brick of the wall, tipping the chair backwards, taking it all in. We are thinking of the day just spent in the gallery and the abstract art we didn't understand; *it could be anything* you say as you place a sieve on your head like a hat, poke dry spaghetti through its holes, we laugh – a translated laugh, a soft drizzle already fading with the barks of the dog outside at the ghost bird that has fallen from its nest.

Lighthouse

after Edward Hopper

In that painting, the dead rabbit is rivered
in a stream of blood that pleats the grass,
the lighthouse stands in a backlash of it all.

At the pet shop with my son, we coo at rabbits
crouching eye level to them; I can hear my breath
in my son's ear, remembering the newborn rabbit

in my grandfather's hands, passing this unbroken heat
into my palms, the way a midwife passed your small
body onto my chest – my world in hesitation,

my son now ensnared in this landscape of animal,
my grandfather, in the headlights of sudden death
the rabbits cowering in the corner of their cage.

There is stillness in that painting, apart from a gust
that flips the thread of a cloud, leaving the blood
between us – we walk out of the pet shop

onto streets of green, cement blistered,
cars rushing as we stroll home holding hands
absorbing the afternoon –

Fox

I could see him far ahead by the side of the road,
curled, unaware of the moving traffic, mid-morning sun
reclining across the concrete sky. His reddening coat
silken with flecks of snow in between the shafts of his fur.
He looked haunting, just lying there, almost flawless.
I watched him in my rear-view mirror, moving further away
until my stare looked back and I heard your breathing –
shallow as the river running through this urban landscape.

In the Pool

The sunlit field of water is ploughed
by my jumping child, her body breaks

its surface. She is learning to reach
the deep end but will not go beyond

what her feet can't touch. She resists
my hands in the ditches of water.

We don't recognise each other,
as she stares – remote, water filling

the island between us. Later, under
the curve of the night, I plunge into

the pool and leap like a salmon upstream
flip onto my back and start counting,

to see how long I can stay like this –
floating with the moon.

Archaeology

We all bury parts of our bodies in the sand,
our children revel in our splintered limbs

for a while we stay like this eyeing the sea,
and our children with their plastic spades

digging and digging for treasure,
their prize, that paragon in the yellow grains.

Red on Maroon

after Mark Rothko

The crushed red in the painting or the curtain
I pull back now and notice how the street lamps
pour their puddles of light. Someone is drunk
in the early hours, their singing is marooned, blood
spilling slowly. I stand watching behind the crushed
red curtain, trying to imagine the war in his body,
its shrapnel for the world to bear, as he staggers,
leans against a wall and waits for the songbird.

Walnut Trees

I rip open the plastic bag, spilling the walnuts
as I pick a handful. Their lunged shape

are your lungs, greying. Far away, the walnut trees
in that back garden stand a little more naked,

empty of people under their boughs in the heat
of a European summer like some photograph.

We were there once with you shelling the walnuts,
your back against the trunk, a stained apron hitched,

shoeless, humming as I climbed into their eaves
and sat eating the skulled bitter walnuts,

their white-sheened skin in my mouth
                         like fallen little gems.

Tomato Picking

They are green, droop with unripened weight.
Just another few days and they'll turn, my husband says,

but they don't. And one afternoon, my son
and I pull off these imperfect fruits, inhaling

their rawness, our fingers becoming the vines,
entangled as we race to see how many we have.

My son says *bad one mummy, good one, bad one*,
though not necessarily in that order;

his mantra is a chorus in which we harvest,
until we have lined our baskets. The autumn light

layers my back as I watch my son: a sparrow
in a new corner of the garden, looking –

Every Morning

I wake up tired, walk downstairs to the kitchen
with our children half-sitting on their chairs

half leaning towards the other side of the day,
breakfast bowls like spaceships, a Lego piece

relinquished, my husband stirring the tea
in that placid manner, metal against porcelain.

Occasionally, I suggest we count the birds
on the bird-print oilcloth, redeem the morning's

blackout and I feather the top of my husband's
head in the same way our legs or the tips of our toes

might feather in bed and say *all right*? –

When our children stay with their grandma,
the kitchen is muffled with ghostly bracken,

I sit in reticence, not because I have nothing to say
but what I do say, we don't recognise

the voice relieved but missing.

Ted

We sit inside the cardboard box,
concealed in its brown frame
as we play being *stuck* in a cave or a
tunnel waiting to be rescued,
our backs now and then slide against
the chalked sound of the cardboard
as we pick at our *provisions* for lunch,
stay close, breathing this in –
the smell of this compressed paper
recalls *Ted*, that lost soldier
I found in a scrap box in a junk shop
that said *cards 50 pence*, his airtight
writing on the back of the photograph:
These are some of the happy boys I am with now.
I imagine his mother reading the sentence
in the black and white of daybreak,
an afternoon retreating like our game
as you scramble out yelling *what next mummy*?

Sign Language

The drawstring of a train gathers this family
into its *vacation*, map-strewn parents haul the luggage

between worn legs, their grown-up children stand
elsewhere, discussing college, essays they have yet to write,

grades – the sign language module one of them is taking
as he explains, *because X is this* and I am trying not to listen,

yet somehow I am dragged deeper into this cloak
of adolescence as their tongues roam a forest.

The father steals a soft glance at his children, amber-warm,
his face inscribed with a code I can nearly interpret,

but still so far from where I sit as I skim
the air of silent language, the gauze of its lineage.

Notes

'Nesting'
What might have been and what has been, point to one end,
Line taken from 'Burnt Norton', the first of T.S. Eliot's *Four Quartets*.

Acknowledgements

Some of these poems have previously appeared in *Lung Jazz: Young British Poets for Oxfam* (Cinnamon Press/Eyewear Publishing, 2012), *Ink Sweat and Tears* and *The Shuffle Anthology 2010-11*. Grateful acknowledgements are duly made to the editors.

This book would not have materialised if it weren't for the support of my husband, whose patience teaches me something new every day, and our family.

A special thank you to the close readers of my work, Alex Lockwood and Tamar Yoseloff, whose continuous support in my writing is invaluable and to Eyewear Publishing for this book and their editors.

 **EYEWEAR** PUBLISHING